CJ
and the
Mysterious
Map

by Kimberly Weinberger
Illustrated by Duendes Del Sur

SCHOLASTIC INC.

New York   Toronto   London   Auckland   Sydney
Mexico City   New Delhi   Hong Kong

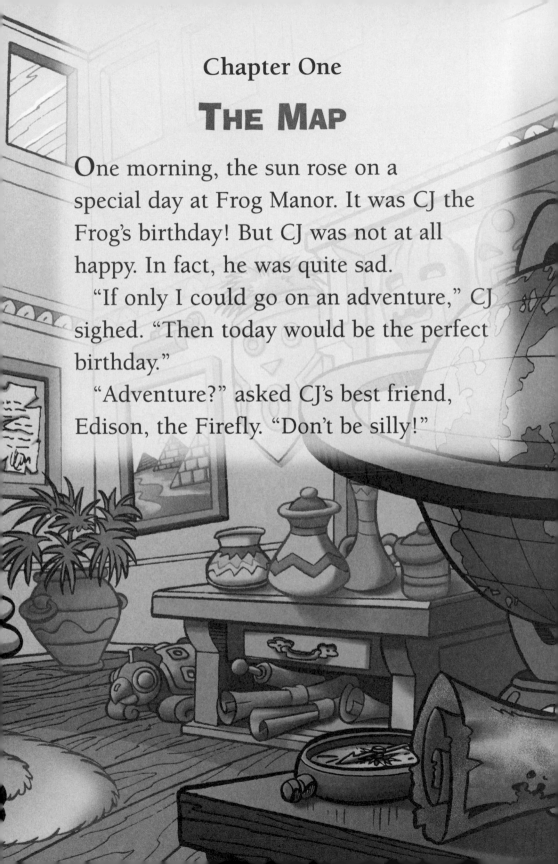

Chapter One

THE MAP

One morning, the sun rose on a special day at Frog Manor. It was CJ the Frog's birthday! But CJ was not at all happy. In fact, he was quite sad.

"If only I could go on an adventure," CJ sighed. "Then today would be the perfect birthday."

"Adventure?" asked CJ's best friend, Edison, the Firefly. "Don't be silly!"

Just then, the doorbell rang.

"Maybe that's a troubled princess who needs my help!" CJ said hopefully.

But when he opened the door, he saw only a letter carrier.

"Some princess," whispered Edison with a chuckle.

Sighing again, CJ looked through the mail.

"Hey!" he shouted excitedly. "Look at this!"

In his hand, he held a wrinkled piece of torn paper.

"It looks like part of a map," said CJ. "And there's a letter, too. *'Follow this map and find great treasure. But BEWARE! Only the bravest will succeed.'"*

"Sounds like a lot of nonsense to me," said Edison. "You just listen to your old pal, Edison. . . ."

But CJ was not listening at all.

"This map could lead to dangerous places, Edison," said CJ, taping the piece of paper into his field notebook.

"Where is my helmet? Where is my compass? A frog has to be ready for anything!"

"Good grief!" said Edison. "We're not going to follow that map, are we? It's silly! It's foolish! It's —"

"An adventure!" shouted CJ joyfully.

And so it was.

Chapter Two
THE SEARCH BEGINS

CJ and Edison set out heading **north** that very morning.

They did not notice, but as they left Frog Manor, a stranger followed. A stranger disguised as a letter carrier!

At last, thought the stranger. *All these weeks of spying on that frog have finally paid off. Little does he know that I, Dr. Listick, have seen that map, too. I'll find the treasure first. Then all of the riches will be mine!*

With a sneaky laugh, Dr. Listick slithered away.

"We're almost there," said CJ.

"And just where would 'there' be?" asked Edison.

"Egypt!" said CJ. "See these triangles on the map? They are symbols for Egypt. See the 'N' on the map? That's the symbol for **north**. According to this map, we need to head just a little farther **north** and we'll reach Egypt. Our compass helps point us in the right direction."

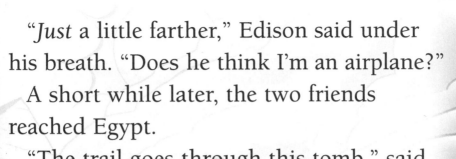

"*Just* a little farther," Edison said under
his breath. "Does he think I'm an airplane?"

A short while later, the two friends
reached Egypt.

"The trail goes through this tomb," said
CJ. "Maybe the rest of the map is hidden
inside. Let's go!"

It was very dark deep inside the tomb.

"How about some light, my friend?" whispered CJ.

Edison turned on his light.

"Oh," cried the firefly, "I wish I hadn't done that!"

In the dim glow, CJ stopped in his tracks. "It's Dr. Listick!" he shouted.

"Surprised to see me?" laughed the snail. "Just wait until you see what else I have in store for you!"

And with that, Dr. Listick slid through a large opening. As CJ and Edison tried to follow, a giant boulder rolled in their path.

"It's blocking our way out!" cried Edison. "What do we do now?"

CJ looked around the tomb.

"I've got it!" he said. "This boulder is only blocking us here on the ground. Look up there. That light is our way out!"

"And how do you suggest we get up there?" asked Edison.

"Teamwork!" said CJ. "I can climb up this wall if you shine your light on it as I go."

Working together, the two friends found their way out of the tomb in no time.

On the wall outside, a strange carving caught CJ's eye.

"Look!" he cried. "It's the next part of the map!"

Quickly, CJ copied the trail in his field notebook.

"We have to catch up with Dr. Listick," he said. "This part of the map says to head **west**. Check the compass! Next stop: Atlantis!"

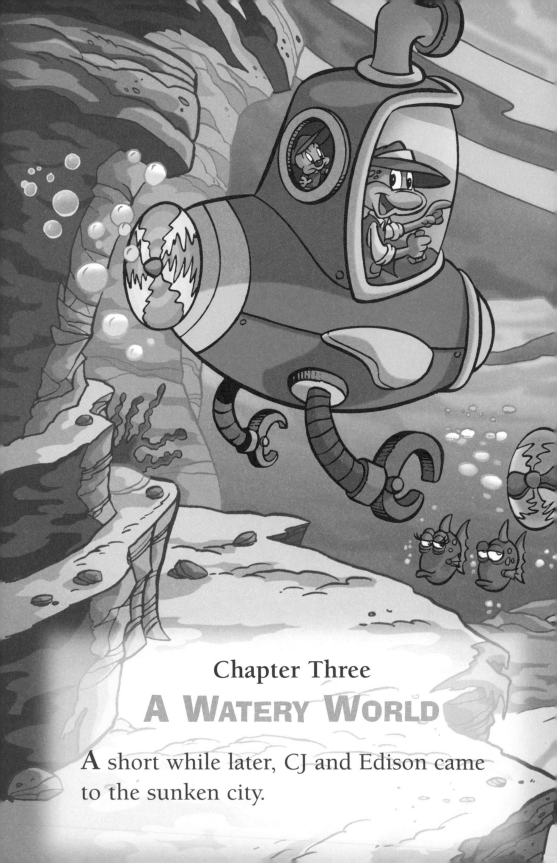

Chapter Three
A WATERY WORLD

A short while later, CJ and Edison came
to the sunken city.

"According to our map, we have to go through that castle," said CJ, pointing ahead.

"Maybe," said a voice over their radio, "but you'll have to go through me first!"

It was Dr. Listick!

"Oh, brother," groaned Edison. "Not again!"

As Dr. Listick started toward them, CJ
hurried to a group of sleeping sea horses.
"What are you doing?" asked Edison.
"It's bubble time!" said CJ.

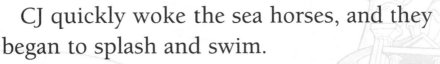

CJ quickly woke the sea horses, and they began to splash and swim.

A huge cloud of bubbles formed right in front of Dr. Listick.

"Drat it all!" said the snail. "I can't see a thing!"

"Look, CJ! I think those seashells are trying to tell us something," said Edison.

"So they are!" CJ agreed.

He added the new directions to his map.

"Get the compass ready! It's time to head **south**," the frog announced. "The ruins of Machu Picchu await!"

Chapter Four
THE GREAT TREASURE

The sun was just starting to set as CJ and Edison reached the site.

"Isn't it beautiful?" said CJ.

Edison had to admit that it was.

"But," said the firefly, "couldn't we have just read about it in a book?"

"Oh, Edison," laughed CJ, "you are a good friend. Who else would come here with me when he'd rather be at home?"

"Someone who has no sense," said Edison, flying ahead.

As they reached the bottom of a mountain, CJ stopped.

"Zounds!" he shouted, pointing at a stone. "The last piece of the map!"

Pulling out his notebook, CJ copied the final path.

"The treasure is **east** of the ruins in a cave. The compass will guide us," he said. "But be careful. These rocks could fall at any time."

CJ and Edison moved forward slowly.

"*Shhh*, my friend," whispered CJ. "Even a loud voice could cause the stones to break apart."

"IS THAT SO?" shouted someone behind them.

They turned to see Dr. Listick as tiny rocks began to fall.

"Let's get out of here!" cried CJ.

"That's the best idea you've had all day," said Edison.

CJ and Edison raced through the falling stones.
"Dr. Listick is still following us,"
CJ said. "There's no time to lose!"
"That must be it," said Edison,
pointing **east** at the cave. "We're almost there!"

All was quiet as the two friends neared
the cave opening.

"Be careful," said CJ. "Danger may be
waiting inside."

"Well, danger is definitely here on the
outside," said Edison, spotting Dr. Listick
in the distance. "Let's go!"

Moving slowly, they passed through the
dark entrance.

"SURPRISE!"

CJ's mouth dropped open.
It was a surprise birthday party for him!

Following them into the cave, Dr. Listick
gasped at the scene.

"A party?" he sneered. "What kind of a
treasure is that?"

Everyone laughed as CJ's enemy stormed out.
"**North**, **south**, **east**, or **west**, you're the
greatest treasures I can think of!" said CJ,
hugging each of his friends.
"But who planned all of this for me?"
The group turned to look at Edison.
The firefly's cheeks grew pink.

"It was nothing," he said. "After all, who wants a sad frog around the house?"

"Edison," said CJ, "you really are the best friend a frog could ask for."

"True," said Edison with a grin. "But what in the world will I ever get for you next year?"